Inger and Lasse Sandberg

# NICHOLAS' FAVORITE PET

A SEYMOUR LAWRENCE BOOK
DELACORTE PRESS / NEW YORK

*Other books by Inger and Lasse Sandberg*

NICHOLAS' RED DAY

LITTLE GHOST GODFREY

THE BOY WITH 100 CARS

NICHOLAS loved animals. He brought home every animal he saw. He wanted his mother to like them too. He put ants in her shoes. He put worms in her flowerpots. And he put a dear little frog on her plate.

But his mother didn't like any of them.

Most of all Nicholas longed for a dog. But when he asked for one, nobody paid any attention. Nicholas didn't understand. Why couldn't he have a pet of his own?

One day, his mother went off to stay with Grandmother, who had hurt her leg. Father stayed behind to look after Nicholas.

# GRANDMOTHER'S BANDAGED LEG

While they were having lunch, Nicholas said: "Daddy, next week I'll be six."

"So you will," said his father.

"Please may I have an elephant for my birthday?" asked Nicholas. His father choked. "An elephant? What for?"

"Think of all the things it
could do," said Nicholas. "Wash
the car, dry Mummy's hair . . .
I could even ride it to school. It
could carry my whole class and
my teacher, too."

His father was not impressed.

"Elephants live in Africa," he said. "They are the biggest animals in the world."

"Oh no," said Nicholas. "Whales are bigger."

"Well, never mind. An elephant weighs as much as six cars."

"What about a baby elephant?" asked Nicholas.

"Even a newborn elephant weighs as much as a fat man. Besides, it would disturb the neighbors with its trumpeting, and when it grew up it would be strong enough to push over the house. Please, Nicholas, think of something else."

"Something smaller?" asked Nicholas.

"Something *much* smaller," said his father.

Nicholas thought. "How about a rhinoceros?" he asked.

His father was speechless.

"Just a tiny one. Please, Daddy. It could plow the garden
with its horn. You'd never have to dig again."

"No thanks," said his father. "I'd rather do the digging
myself."

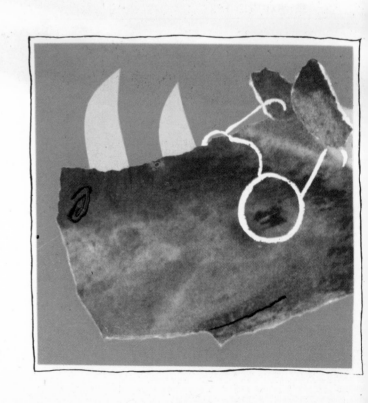

"Anyway, they're much too wild. A cross rhinoceros could knock down a *train*."

"It wouldn't knock us down," said Nicholas. "We'd be its friends."

"It might not recognize us. Rhinoceroses are very nearsighted," said his father.

"We could buy it some glasses."

"But the rhinoceros has a friend already, a little bird who pecks the bugs out of its thick skin. Sometimes the bugs bother the rhinoceros so much that it rolls in the mud to get rid of them. So you see, it needs the little bird much more than it needs us."

"Oh well," said Nicholas, "if it has a friend already, I'll have a hippopotamus instead."

"Impossible," said his father. "Where would we keep it? Hippos need a lot of warm water. They eat, sleep, and play underwater and only come up now and then, to breathe. You wouldn't see much of your hippo."

"Do they get cross like rhinoceroses?"
"If you met a mother hippopotamus with her babies she would probably get very cross."

"If I had a hippopotamus," said Nicholas, "I'd soon learn how to swim."

"That would be cheating," said his father. "You keep
practicing with your water wings."

Next morning, at breakfast, his father said: "Well, Nicholas, have you thought about what you'd like for your birthday?"

"Yes, Daddy. I'd like something cuddly."

"That's more like it," said his father.

"A nice, big, cuddly, yellow lion."

"Good grief!" cried his father. "Not a lion! What on earth would we do with a lion?"

"That's easy," said Nicholas. "It would be our watchdog, and think how good it would be at catching mice and besides, Mummy could use it as a foot-warmer and . . ."

"Just a minute, Nicholas," said his father. "It would cost far too much to buy meat for such a big animal. Let me tell you about lions. They live in Africa with a whole lot of other lions —brothers, sister, uncles, aunts—and they're not afraid of anything. Even the giraffe, the tallest animal in the world, runs away from them. The father lion has a big mane and people call him 'the king of the animals.'"

"That wasn't what I wanted to know," said Nicholas. "Can I have one or not?"

"You cannot," said his father. "Let's go for a walk."

Behind the house was a meadow, and beyond the meadow, a little forest. Walking through the fresh-smelling trees made Nicholas feel happy again.

"I promise I won't ask for any more big animals," he told his father. "What about a snake?"

"A snake? Poor Mummy! She's so afraid of snakes," said his father.

"Maybe she'll change her mind if she sees how helpful they are. A boa would be best. I could use it as a swing, Mummy could use it when she does the cleaning, and it would help you paint the sitting room. Or what about a crocodile? We could keep it in that old bathtub in the cellar."

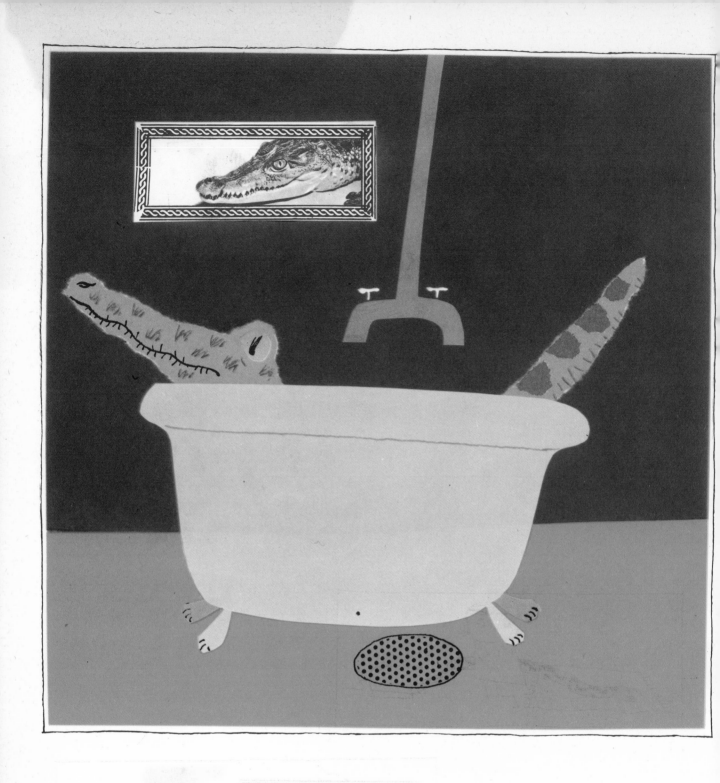

"Crocodiles wouldn't like cellars. They like warm places where they can lie in the sun all day, having their teeth cleaned by a helpful little bird. Sometimes they dive into rivers or lakes to eat fish or little water animals or stones."

"Stones?"

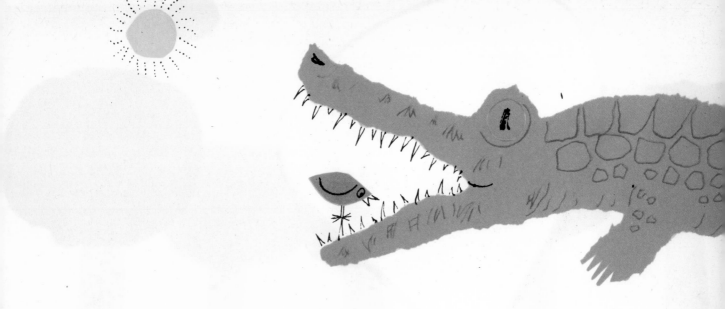

"Yes, the stones help grind up the food in their stomachs. Crocodiles can't chew very well in spite of all those teeth."

"Do crocodiles have many children?"

"A mother crocodile lays about fifty eggs in a hole in the ground. Then the sun shines on the eggs and fifty tiny crocodiles start to hatch."

"Fifty? Then there just wouldn't be room in the bathtub," said Nicholas.

He was silent. As they walked through the woods, he thought about the snakes he would like to have—not the most poisonous ones like rattlesnakes or the world's biggest crushing snakes, like pythons. But he did wish he could have a basket full of snakes to take to school.

Then he could pull out a cobra and say: "Come down off
that shelf, Miss Simpson. Don't be afraid. My cobra's fangs
were taken out in India." Or—

"Look at the tame viper I've got curled around my arm. She's called Mary Jane."

All of a sudden Nicholas heard something rustling in the grass.

"Help!" he yelled. "A black mamba!"

"Don't be silly," said his father, peering down. "It's only a harmless grass snake."

"Are you sure it isn't a viper?" cried Nicholas.

"Of course I'm sure," said his father. "This snake has a round black spot in the middle of its eyes instead of a slit. And look at those two yellow patches! All grass snakes have those."

Nicholas calmed down. Maybe he didn't want a snake for a pet, after all.

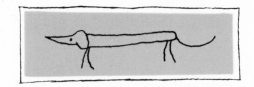

At last it was Nicholas' birthday. Grandmother's leg was better and his mother was home again. Nicholas lay in bed, waiting. Finally the door opened and in came his mother and father with a heap of presents.

"Happy birthday!" said his mother.

"Thank you, thank you," mumbled Nicholas as he unwrapped the packages and found a pair of mittens, a flashlight, and a large book about animals.

"You'll find all the animals you asked for in that book," said his father.

"But what would be your very favorite pet?" asked his mother.

"A DOG," sighed Nicholas. "A dog of my own."

"You never told me you wanted a dog," said his father. "What kind of dog would you like?"

Nicholas looked at all the pictures of dogs in his book. Then he said: "If I could have a dog, any kind would do."

And then—imagine!—his mother went into the kitchen and came back with a basket. In the basket was a little dachshund puppy, with big, round feet and brown eyes.

"Here he is!" said his mother. "We'll help you look after him, but he's your very own puppy."

Nicholas picked up the puppy and hugged him, and whispered in his ear: "I'll look after you every minute. You can sleep on my bed; you can have lots of food and plenty of bones to chew. And every day we'll go for a walk in the woods. Won't that be fun?"

And that's how Nicholas got his favorite pet.

He didn't get an elephant

or a rhinoceros

or a hippopotamus

or a lion

or a snake

or a crocodile

but he got what he wanted more than anything
else in the world—a puppy of his very own.